What Does a Princess Really Look Like?

By Mark Loewen   Illusrated by Ed Pokoj

Virginia

Published in the United States by BQB Publishing
(an imprint of Boutique of Quality Books Publishing Company)
www.bqbpublishing.com

Printed in the United States of America

978-1-945448-17-1 (h)
978-1-945448-18-8 (e)

Library of Congress Control Number: 2018938438

Cover and interior illustrations: Ed Pokoj
Interior Design Setup: Robin Krauss, www.bookformatters.com
Editor: Olivia Swenson

To Zoe, the most courageous girl I know, for teaching me how to be brave like a girl! And to Leo, for all the love you brought to my life. I can't imagine it without you.

— M.L.

For my Parents, my Brother, my Sister, and my Wife for all the support you have given me over the years.

— E.P.

This is Chloe.

She loves princesses and ballerinas.

Every day, she twirls and leaps

from room to room like a

ballerina princess dancing

in her castle.

Sometimes her two dads dance along.

But today the house is quiet.

In her room, Chloe is working on a special project.

She is creating her very own Princess Ballerina.

Chloe wants her princess to be **perfect**.

She makes a circle for the head.

"Inside our head is where our smarts are," she thinks to herself, "and this princess is very smart."

Now she needs hair.

Chloe digs into her art supply box and finds colorful yarn.

clunk

Bump

"Princesses have **beautiful** hair," she says.

8

She pauses, glue dripping onto the floor. "Actually, being a princess is about more than looking pretty," Chloe realizes.

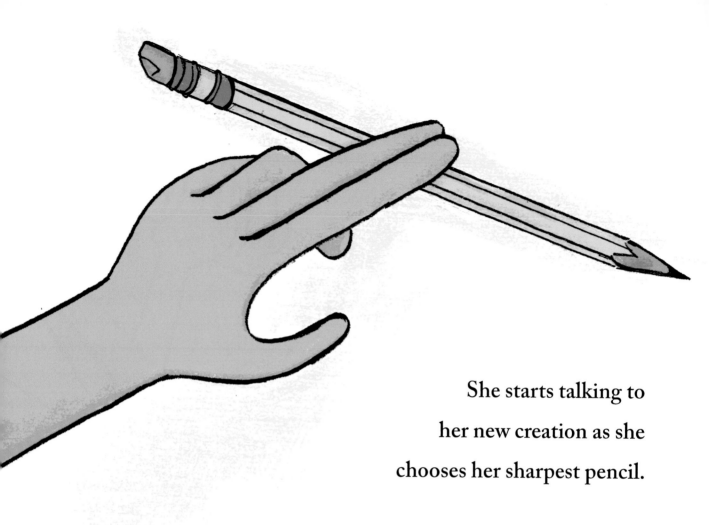

She starts talking to
her new creation as she
chooses her sharpest pencil.

I will give you the best
eyes and ears. Princesses
are very observant.

"They notice things others can't see.

Lots of people come to you when they need help.

And you have to listen carefully to figure out exactly

what they need - so you can help them!"

And now I will give you a mouth. You need a voice to speak kind words. But you also need to tell people when you are feeling frustrated.

And you must speak up when something is wrong.

Chloe remembers a time when
her friend Ellie hurt her feelings.
Using her own voice, Chloe asked
Ellie to stop.

Chloe sighs. Being a princess
is not always an easy job.

But then, her eyes light up as she thinks of what comes next.

a Crown!

She glues beautiful jewels and beads to the princess's head.

You wear this crown so everyone knows you make big decisions for your kingdom.

Chloe takes a look at the finished crown.

"Wow! You look so important,"
she says, impressed. "But we're not
done yet!"

"Your neck holds your head tall." Chloe knows that when she stands tall, she feels brave.

Ooh, and your arms!
Yes, you are strong!

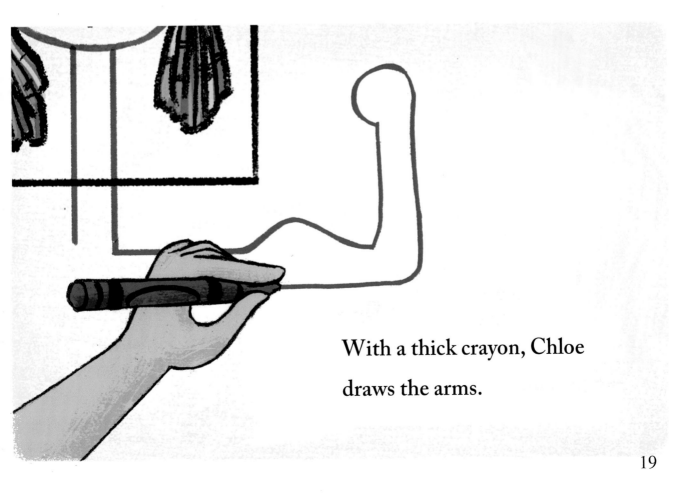

With a thick crayon, Chloe
draws the arms.

When you know what you want, nothing can stop you!

Using a large sheet of pink paper, Chloe cuts out the shape of a dress and glues it on her princess. Then she notices . . .

Oh No!

. . . the dress is crooked!

mmmff!

She tries to straighten the dress, but the glue is too strong. The dress stays crooked. "Oh gosh," says Chloe.

You were supposed to be **perfect!**

23

At that moment, Daddy and Papa peek their heads around the door.

Chloe is worried about the crooked dress. She doesn't want her dads to see her work of art with a mistake!

Daddy and Papa enter her room
and look at Chloe's princess in awe.
"Wow," says Daddy impressed.
"And look," cheers Papa.
"The dress looks like
she is dancing!"

Wow!

Look!

26

"Of course!" realizes Chloe. She feels relieved and laughs out loud.

This princess LOVES to dance!

27

Princesses can look all kinds of ways. They can be artists, ninjas, explorers, builders, or anything they like.

Draw your own princess here:

Please share your princess with us.

Post your picture with the hashtags

#whatdoesaprincessreallylooklike #bravelikeagirl

About the Author and Illustrator

Mark Loewen is a phychotherapist and a dad. He was born in Asuncion, Paraguay and moved to the United States to pursue his counseling career. He met the love of his life in Richmond, Virginia. A few years later, they became dads through open adoption. Becoming a father to a  girl opened Mark's eyes to the challenges many girls and women face in today's world. *"What Does a Princess Really Look Like"* is his first children's book. He is also the Founder of Brave Like A Girl, an organization that helps girls overcome challenges by tapping into their courage and strength.

Ed Pokoj is an illustrator and animator. He lives with his wife in Richmond, Virginia. He aims to make everyday life more fun and exciting by creating whimsical and colorful illustrations for the world to enjoy.